Mystery of the Missing Jars

Written by Maria Grace Dateno, FSP
Illustrated by Paul Cunningham

Pauline
BOOKS & MEDIA
Boston

Library of Congress Cataloging-in-Publication Data

Dateno, Maria Grace.
  Mystery of the missing jars / written by Maria Grace Dateno, FSP ;
illustrated by Paul Cunningham.
      pages cm. -- (Gospel time trekkers ; 4)
  Summary: Siblings Hannah, Caleb, and Noah, aged six through ten,
travel through time and space to Capernaum where they meet Jairus and
his daughter, Sarah, whom Jesus raised from the dead, but get in trouble
when Caleb is accused of stealing.
  ISBN-13: 978-0-8198-4922-9
  ISBN-10: 0-8198-4922-7
  [1. Time travel--Fiction. 2. Brothers and sisters--Fiction. 3. Raising of
Jairus' daughter (Miracle)--Fiction. 4. Jesus Christ--Miracles--Fiction.
5. Christian life--Fiction.] I. Cunningham, Paul, (Paul David), 1972-
illustrator. II. Title.
  PZ7.D2598Mys 2014
  [Fic]--dc23

                          2013002499

The Scripture quotations contained herein are from the *New Revised
Standard Version Bible: Catholic Edition*, copyright © 1989, 1993, Division
of Christian Education of the National Council of the Churches of Christ
in the United States of America. Used by permission. All rights reserved.

Cover design by Mary Joseph Peterson, FSP

Cover art by Paul Cunningham

Published by Pauline Books & Media, 50 Saint Pauls Avenue, Boston, MA
02130-3491

Printed in the U.S.A.

MOMJ KSEUSAHUDNHA5-261066 4922-7

www.pauline.org

Pauline Books & Media is the publishing house of the Daughters of
St. Paul, an international congregation of women religious serving the
Church with the communications media.

3 4 5 6 7 8 9   20 19 18 17 16

To my siblings—
George, Jennie, Elizabeth,
Sarah, and Emily
—and to our childhood memories
(even if only some of us have them).

Contents

Chapter One

The Smashed Rocket

"It's not fair!" I yelled as I came into the house.

"Caleb, calm down and tell me what you're angry about," Mom said.

"I'm not angry! I'm just so mad that Kevin said he wouldn't mess up this time and he did."

"What did he mess up?"

"Our rocket for the Space Adventures Science Fair project! We've been working on it for ages. I know we could have won a prize. And now he's ruined it!"

"Maybe it can be fixed," said Mom.

"No, it can't!" I said.

"You didn't even see it," said Hannah, as she came in the door behind me. She had been visiting her friend, who was Kevin's older sister. "Neither did I. I'm just telling you what Kevin's sister said. It's in pieces and kind of smashed. But it might not be his fault, Caleb. Their baby sister might have done it."

"Why do people always blame the youngest one?" asked Noah. He's six and is the youngest in our family.

"You're not helping, guys!" I said.

"Well, according to you, there's nothing anyone can do to help," said Hannah. "Come on, Noah. Let's go see if there are any tomatoes that are ripe."

"What am I going to do, Mom?" I asked, after they had left. "The fair is this Tuesday!"

"The first thing is to wait until you see the damage yourself. It might not be as bad as you think."

How could "in pieces and kind of smashed" not be as bad as I think! I thought.

Just then, my mom's cell phone beeped at her, and she looked at the text message. They're almost always from my dad.

"Hey, Caleb. Dad wants you guys in the workshop to try out that new 3-D puzzle he's working on."

"Sure!" I said and jumped up to head out the door. It was amazing how I felt so much better so quickly.

My dad's workshop is next door to the house. It's where he makes furniture and toys out of wood, which is his job. He's starting to teach me woodworking.

I was halfway across the yard to Dad's workshop when I heard Hannah and Noah coming back from the garden. I was going to hurry into the workshop by myself and not tell them that Dad had called for us. That way I could be the first one to try out the new toy. But something made me change my mind. I stopped and turned toward them.

"Hannah! Noah!" I called. "Dad wants us to try out something."

"Oh, yay!" said Noah. They hurried over and we headed toward the workshop.

That's when something amazing happened.

It wasn't the first time it had happened. (It was actually the fourth time.) But this time we weren't trying to make it happen. We weren't talking about it, or even thinking about it.

But it happened anyway.

Chapter Two

Exploring the Market

The air got thick and we moved slowly, as if we were trying to walk through water. And then, the air was back to normal, but *we* were changed.

"It's happened again!" yelled Noah. "We're back in the time of Jesus!"

He jumped up and down in his light brown tunic. I had one like it—it was a sort of robe with a tie around the waist. Hannah's was similar, but had decorations around the neck, so you could tell it was for a girl. Whenever we went back to the time of Jesus, our clothes became like this—it was what everyone was wearing.

Hannah and I just stared at each other. I couldn't believe we were here again. The first time it happened, when we ended up in Bethlehem, we had been riding our bikes. The last time we were just starting to weed the garden. This time we were just *walking*.

"Wow," I said. "This is amazing. How in the world did it happen again?" I looked around and realized that we were right outside a village.

"This looks a little like Gennesaret," said Hannah. That was the village we were in last time.

"I can smell the sea!" said Noah. It was called the Sea of Galilee, but it was really a big lake. Last time, I went on a fishing boat on the lake at night. It was fun, but ended up being kind of dangerous.

"But we've never gone to the same place twice," I said. "So it probably isn't Gennesaret."

"True," said Hannah. "Let's go walk around and see."

We saw a few people ahead of us and followed them. We came to an open area among the buildings that seemed to be the market.

"This definitely isn't Gennesaret," said Hannah.

"How do you know?" asked Noah.

"I went with Rebecca to the market there, and it was smaller than this," said Hannah. Rebecca was a girl we met last time. She talked a lot, but she and her family were very nice.

One table had baskets of fruit on it. I was looking at the fruit when I heard two people talking at another table nearby. There was a man selling something in little jars. He had a striped tunic that was bright red and white. His mantle, which was like a scarf that he wore around his shoulders, was purple-blue. I didn't remember seeing anyone else wearing such colorful clothes the other times we had come. Another man came up and started talking to him.

"Good morning to you, my friend," said the second man. "I am an official of the town of Capernaum. I am doing an inspection this morning. Please show me your weights and scale."

I was behind the merchant, so I couldn't see his face. But he didn't sound upset that there was an inspection. I was curious about what was being inspected, so I stayed to watch.

"Certainly, sir," said the merchant. "Here are my weights."

He put some little metal shapes on the table. The official held each of them up and looked at them closely, then set them back down. They looked like flat metal game pieces of different sizes.

The official also had a thing that I guess was the scale. It had two bowls hanging from a bar at the top. The official held it up in the air, so that the bowls were hanging down evenly. He put one of the little metal things from the merchant in one bowl and it went down like a seesaw with only one person on it. Then he took another weight from his own bag and put it in the other bowl. The two bowls became even. He did this several times with different weights.

"That is satisfactory," said the official. "Now I will check *your* scale."

He did the same thing over again, but with the merchant's scale instead of his own.

"Thank you, all is in order," said the official.

"Of course," said the merchant. "I am an honest man, and I am happy to do business here in Capernaum."

The official walked away. Then a woman came up and began looking at the containers.

"These are the finest spices you will find, and the pottery jars are especially made to keep the spices fresh for a long time," said the merchant.

"I do need some dried spices," said the woman.

"Ah, here I have some very fine mint and dill. Smell that," said the merchant, picking up a little jar and pulling a little bag out of it. He held the bag for the woman to smell.

She seemed happy with it and decided to buy some. But when the merchant told her the price, she said it was way too expensive.

Noah and Hannah came up behind me at that point.

"Hey, Caleb," said Noah. "What are you doing? We were looking at some of the things they're selling."

"Yeah, me, too," I said.

"It's funny to go shopping outdoors, isn't it?" said Noah.

"Yes, it's like a farmers' market," I said.

I turned back to look at the merchant and saw that the woman must have decided to buy some of the spices after all. She stood waiting as the merchant held up his scale. He put the little bag of spices in one of the bowls. The scale tipped down on that side, like a see-saw.

"What's he doing?" asked Noah.

"I think he's weighing that thing the lady's buying," said Hannah.

"Yeah, you'll see—he's going to put one of those little metal things on the other side, to see how much she should pay," I said.

But the merchant didn't do that. Instead, he reached into a bag that was hanging from his belt. He looked over toward the official who was doing an inspection a few tables away. Then he pulled a weight out of the bag and put it on the other side of the scale. They became even. Then the lady gave the merchant some coins. He put the bag back into the little jar and gave it to her. She thanked him and walked away.

"That's odd," I said. "I thought he'd use one of the weights on the table."

But Hannah and Noah had turned and were walking along the edge of the market. I left and ran after them.

Chapter Three

A New Friend

"Hey! Let's look around and see if Levi and his dad are here!" Noah was saying when I caught up with them.

Levi was the boy we met on our second trip. His dad was a traveling merchant and Levi went with him from town to town. They sold pots and pans and other things made of metal.

"It's not very likely, Noah," said Hannah. "But we can look."

"He'd be really surprised to see us!" I said. At the end of each of our adventures, we had ust suddenly found ourselves back in our own time. So we didn't even say good-bye to Levi. He probably wondered what had happened to us.

The market was not that big, so before long we could tell that Levi was not there.

"Hey, I'm hungry," said Noah. "Too bad we don't have any money."

I was hungry, too, but we never had any money when we went back in time. Even if there had been something in our pockets before, nothing would come with us.

"Look at those people over there," said Hannah.

"What are they—Oh! That man gave them money," said Noah.

"They're begging, right?" I asked, and Hannah nodded.

We walked by the people begging, and I saw that some of them couldn't walk or couldn't see. Most of them looked sick. One of them, an old man with white curly hair, was staring at us as we walked by.

"Too bad we don't have any money," said Noah. "We could share it with them."

I was just about to say something about finding someone to share with *us*, but suddenly I caught sight of a girl walking in our direction. She had long, wavy, dark brown hair, and she was smiling as she walked. She looked about the same age as Hannah, or a little older. Most importantly, she was carrying a basket.

"Hey, I wonder if she has some lunch in there," I said. "Let's go talk to her."

We didn't need to go talk to her, though, because she came up to us and talked first.

"Hello," she said. "Who are you? I do not remember seeing any of you before."

"Hello, I'm Hannah, and these are my brothers."

"I'm Caleb," I said. "And this is Noah."

"I'm Sarah," the girl replied. "You're lucky to have brothers, Hannah. I don't have any. Nor sisters."

"Maybe you could help us, Sarah," said Hannah. "What town is this?"

"It's called Capernaum," she said. "Are you

traveling with your parents? Where are you going?"

We never knew what to say when people in Jesus's time asked us that.

"No, we're traveling by ourselves," I said. "But our parents won't be worried about us."

"You look like you might be hungry. I came to the market for my mother. Come home with me and I will get you something to eat."

People at the time of Jesus were usually very nice to strangers and travelers. During our adventures, so many people had given us food and a place to stay.

"Thank you, Sarah!" said Hannah. "Are you sure it's all right?"

"Of course!" said Sarah. "Are you staying long in Capernaum?"

"We're hoping to see Jesus," I said. "Do you know if he will be coming here soon?"

"Oh! I hope so! I would love to see him and talk to him again!"

"You talked to him?" exclaimed Noah.

"He was here?" asked Hannah. "When was that?"

"He used to be here a lot! But it has been a few months now. We have heard that he was in the area a few weeks ago, but he has not come back to our town yet. I do not know why—I hope it is not because of me . . . ." she said. Her pretty smile disappeared.

Chapter Four

Sarah's Story

"What do you mean?" I asked.

"It is a long story," she answered. "I can tell you as you eat."

We all followed her down the street. She pointed to one house as we walked by.

"That is the house of Anna, who is the mother-in-law of one of the disciples of Jesus," said Sarah. "Jesus stays there whenever he is in Capernaum."

We continued around the corner and down another street, to a little house. It was made of black stone, very much like the house of

Rebecca's family that we saw on our last adventure. This kind of house was really two or three buildings with an open space in the middle, called a courtyard.

"Imma! I am back from the market!" Sarah said as she entered the house.

We had learned on our other trips that "Imma" means "Mom" and "Abba" means "Dad."

We followed slowly and stood just inside the door. There was a woman there. She had a white tunic with a fancy red belt around the waist. Her mantle was around her shoulders, hanging down on each side. It had some red decorations on the edge.

"Sarah, my darling!" said the woman, smiling. She came over and gave Sarah a big hug and kiss.

It seemed funny to me that her mom would act so happy to see her. Sarah had just been to the market, but from the way her mother acted, it seemed as if she had just come back from a long trip.

"Imma, here are Hannah and Caleb and Noah."

Sarah's mother told us her name was Judith and her husband's name was Jairus. The way she said his name, "Jairus," rhymed with "virus."

"They are traveling all by themselves and are hungry," said Sarah. "Can we have something to eat?"

"Certainly, my darling. You can all go into the courtyard and sit in the shade. I will bring you some bread and cheese and we have grapes and some fig cake, too."

"Thank you, Imma," said Sarah. She brought us outside and into the courtyard. On the sunny side, there were plants growing up the wall. I was pretty sure what I saw hanging from the vines were cucumbers. There were also some flower pots with small green plants growing in them.

Sarah was very kind and helped us sit down on little cushions in the shady area. Then she smiled.

"I am going to tell you my story now. You asked why I said that maybe Jesus had not come back to our town because of me. I did not mean because of me, exactly, but because he is so famous around here now because of what he did for me."

"Oh!" said Hannah suddenly. "Oh! The daughter of Jairus!"

"Yes," said Sarah, nodding. "I see that maybe you have heard my story."

I still didn't know what they were talking about, so I was glad when Noah piped up and said, "I haven't heard it."

"Well, now you will," said Sarah, smiling at Noah. "I was very sick, and then I was, well . . . anyway, I do not actually remember what happened, but this is what my father and mother have told me.

"I was sick with a high fever. I had been in bed for days and I remember the doctor coming, and my mother and father crying when he left. I think he must have said there was nothing he could do to help me.

"After that, I do not remember anything. But my father decided he would go ask Jesus for help. My father works as a potter, but he is an important man in this town because he is also an official of the synagogue."

"What is an official of the synagogue?" I asked. Hannah frowned at me, but I thought it was a good question.

"You know, the officials are the ones who arrange the service on the Sabbath and choose who will do the readings. My father is much respected here in Capernaum."

I still wasn't sure what she was talking about, but I didn't ask any more questions.

"He ran to find Jesus," Sarah continued, "who was visiting our town and preaching. He fell down on his knees before Jesus and said, 'Please come and lay your hands on my little daughter. She is near death. Please come and save her.'

"And Jesus got up and came with him. My father was so happy. He said he wanted Jesus to run with him back to our house. But then, while they were coming—and a whole crowd of people, too, since lots of people followed Jesus wherever he went—someone else stopped him for help! Abba said he was so upset that Jesus was distracted by some other sick person. It was a woman who obviously was not even close to dying. Why stop to help her when a child was at death's door?"

At this point in the story, Sarah's mom came out with a whole bunch of food. There was bread and cheese, but also lots of other stuff.

"Here you go. You must all be so hungry. Sarah, dear, come and let me know if you need more of anything."

"Thank you, Imma! I am telling them my story about Jesus."

"Thank you," said Hannah.

"Yay!" said Noah, grabbing a piece of bread. As we ate, Sarah continued her story.

"So, Jesus stopped and healed this woman who was sick. And meanwhile, my father was so worried, thinking how he could get Jesus to come more quickly, before it was too late.

"Finally, Jesus was done with the lady and he turned to continue to our house. But at that moment, a man came up and told my father, 'Do not bother the teacher any longer. Your daughter has already died.'"

Chapter Five

Dead—then Alive!

"You *died*?" I exclaimed. It was hard to believe. Sarah was sitting there with her sparkling eyes. She was so pretty and so alive. How could she have been dead?

"Oh! Your poor father!" said Hannah.

"Jesus heard what the person had said. He looked at my father and said, 'Do not be afraid. Just believe.' He made the whole crowd stay behind and he came with my father and some of his disciples to our house. There were already people mourning outside the door, and you know what a commotion *that* is. Jesus told them to stop because I was not dead, only asleep. And everybody laughed at him!"

"Why did they laugh?" asked Noah. "It was sad, not funny."

"They laughed at Jesus, making fun of him as if he were stupid, because they knew I was dead, and only someone stupid would not be able to tell the difference between someone asleep and someone dead. A sleeping person is still breathing!

"So, then Jesus made everyone leave the house except my mother and father and the disciples he had with him. Then he came into the room where I was lying on the bed. He took my hand and said, 'Little girl, arise.'

"This part I remember well. I opened my eyes and saw a man looking down at me. I will never forget the way he smiled, with a look of victory, when he saw my eyes open.

"He was holding my hand, and when I sat up, he helped me get out of the bed and walk. I looked around and saw my mother with her eyes wide open and my father, too. My father collapsed into a chair and started sobbing. There were two or three other men there that I did not know. I wanted to ask for something to eat because I felt starving, but I felt a little shy to ask in front of those strangers.

"Then Jesus said to my mother, 'Give her something to eat!' And I was so glad. My parents barely had time to thank him and then he left. My mother got me something and I never had such delicious food in my entire life."

"Wow, that's amazing, Sarah," said Hannah. "I have heard your story before, but I didn't know that was you when we first met."

"So you don't remember what it felt like to be dead?" I asked.

"Caleb," said Hannah, frowning at me.

"What?" I said. "I was just wondering. I mean, I've never met anyone who was dead before."

"Ca-leb!"

"It is all right, Hannah. I have had people ask me that before. I really do not remember anything. I am just so happy to be alive. Every day of life is a gift from God! And my parents thank God every day for me."

"Yeah, I was kind of surprised how your mother acted when she saw you—like she hadn't seen you in a long time," I said.

"Having a chance at a new life changes the way you see things," said Sarah. "I know it has for me, and for my parents as well."

"Why did you say that Jesus might not come back here because of you?" asked Noah.

"Oh, I meant that he has become so famous for raising me from the dead. When he shows up he will be completely overwhelmed by the crowds. Even though he has not come back here yet, lots of people travel to whatever place they hear he's in."

"Oh, we want to know if he is anywhere nearby," said Hannah.

"If he is, we will hear about it," said Sarah. "Do not worry about that."

I had been eating the whole time she was talking, so I was pretty full, but I still kept eating these round, white things that tasted like pickles.

"These are good," I said. "What are they?"

"Pickled onions," said Sarah.

"Oh," I said, thinking that if my mom had said, *Here, Caleb, try these pickled onions*, I would have said *No, yuck*!

Chapter Six

Smoke, Fire, and Mud

When Sarah left to take the food and dishes inside, we immediately started talking about what to do.

"Do you think we could stay here?" Noah asked. "They seem nice, and they don't have a lot of kids so there should be room."

"Don't we want to go find Jesus?" I said.

"Well, Jesus might come here," said Hannah. "And even if he doesn't, the people of the town will know when he's going to be nearby."

"I'm glad we came here. It was really neat to hear her story," said Noah. "Imagine

29

waking up from being dead and Jesus is standing there!"

"Let's ask her if there's someone who would know when Jesus comes to a town or village that we could walk to," I said.

Just then, Sarah came back out.

"Would you like to go see my father's workshop?" she asked. "It is just down the street."

"Sure!" I said.

"He cannot have it here at the house, but it is not far to walk," Sarah explained. "Potters need to work a little bit outside the village because of the smoke."

"Smoke?" I said. "I thought pottery was made from clay."

"Yes, so he also needs to be near a place where he can dig up the clay. And he needs a water source for mixing with the clay and to wash up."

As she was talking, we left the courtyard and walked down the street. We were walking out of the village, away from the Sea of Galilee.

"I still don't get why there's smoke," I said.

"Oh, is it because of the kiln?" asked Hannah.

"The what?" said Noah.

"The kiln is a kind of oven where the pottery pieces are baked and hardened. It creates a lot of smoke," said Sarah. She pointed to a thing that looked like a very short house with a round roof. "That's my father's kiln. He's not firing anything right now. And here's his workshop."

We walked toward the building. We saw that there was a big opening on one side, bigger than a doorway. There was a man sitting there, working. Because of the opening, anyone walking by could see what he was doing. On each side of the opening, there were small tables with jugs and bowls and pots on them. I guessed that people could buy those.

"Hello, Abba!" said Sarah.

The man looked up and smiled big.

"Hello, my darling!" he said. "I would come to greet you and your friends if my hands were not full of clay."

"That's all right, Abba. May we watch you for a little while?"

"Certainly, Sarah. Who are these children?"

"This is Hannah, this is Caleb, and the youngest is Noah. They are traveling and we are giving them hospitality."

"Excellent, my dear! I need to make one more jug. Then I will clean up and we will go home for the evening."

I had seen a picture of a person making pottery on a wheel, but I hadn't ever seen anyone do it. We stood there and watched as Jairus took a big lump of clay, which was reddish-brown, and put it in the middle of a flat wooden circle. Then he did something with his feet to make the wheel spin around. I couldn't see exactly what he was doing.

As the wheel spun around, he put his hands on the clay and pressed with his fingers. The clay became a smooth lump. Then, gradually, the clay got taller and then a hole formed down the middle, like a mug.

Suddenly, the clay kind of jerked and crumpled up. Jairus stopped the wheel. He didn't look upset that his jug got ruined. He took the clay and smashed it into a lump again. Then he stuck it back onto the middle of the wheel, and started the wheel spinning again. Then he began to shape the clay like before.

We stood watching until Jairus finished the jug. It was tall and most of it was chubby, but the top was skinny and had a small hole.

"Wow," said Noah quietly. "I wish I could do something like that."

I didn't say anything, but I was itching to get my hands on some clay myself.

"What's he doing now?" asked Noah.

We watched as Jairus took a piece of string tied to two sticks. Holding the sticks like handles, he pulled the string tight and started to slide it underneath the jug.

"That's how he cuts the piece off the wheel without smashing it or making it uneven," said Sarah.

Jairus then took the jug and carefully sat it on a ledge.

"I wonder what the clay feels like," I said to myself.

Hannah was standing next to me and heard.

"It looks like mud," she said. "So it probably just feels like mud."

"That's what I was thinking," I said. "Don't you wish you could squish it with your hands?"

Hannah looked at me and rolled her eyes. Maybe not.

Chapter Seven

Five Little Jars

Jairus came out of his workshop and washed his hands and arms in a big tub of water. As he was cleaning up, I noticed someone watching us from behind a bush near the path we had come by. It was the old man with white curly hair who had been begging in the marketplace.

I was going to point him out to Hannah, but Jairus had finished washing up.

"Come inside!" he said. So we all went into the workshop.

"Welcome," he said. "Sarah, my dear, I am glad that you met and welcomed these children to our home."

"Thank you, sir," said Hannah.

"How does the wheel go around?" asked Noah. "Is it electric?"

"Is it what?" said Jairus.

"Nothing. Never mind," I said. Noah always asked confusing questions. "What other kinds of things do you make?"

Jairus laughed a little. "I make what people need," he said. "This is Capernaum. It is a fishing town, and fishermen mostly need simple pots, jugs, bowls, and dishes. But I like to use my skill to make some smaller vessels of fine clay, too. It is not often that I am asked to make something special!"

Jairus looked very pleased with himself. He pointed toward a small table to the side of the workshop. There were five tiny jars there. They looked much smoother than the other pots nearby. And the top edge of the small jars was very thin, with a blue stripe around it. Near the bottom there were more blue decorations. I didn't know what they would be for. They were too small for putting something to drink in.

"These are specially made perfume jars. I fired them yesterday and am very happy with the results. They are commissioned by a special customer, and I will be paid well. Making things of the fine clay is a great deal of work."

Sarah looked closely at the jars, but did not touch them, so we didn't either.

"They are very lovely," said Hannah.

"And to answer Noah's question about how the wheel goes around: you can look down here where my feet are on another wheel, connected to the wheel on top. I spin it around with my feet. My friend who is a carpenter has made it well balanced. So it spins very smoothly." He gave it a spin to show us.

"Can I try to make something?" asked Noah.

Jairus laughed.

"No, son," he said. "Even if you were going to come learn pot-making from me, you would not start with the wheel. There are many other steps before I throw the clay on the wheel."

"Like what?" asked Noah.

"First I must dig up the clay. It has lots of small stones and twigs in it. These must be picked out. I knead the clay to make it smooth. I mix it with water and wait for the mixture to settle. I use only the top part. And if I am going to make something very fine, I have to do that several times before the clay is ready. It takes much longer to prepare that kind of fine clay."

"What are these?" I asked, pointing to another table with some other jugs on it. They were a lot like the one he had just finished, except they each had two handles near the skinny top part.

"Those are all jugs I made today and yesterday. They are drying."

"When will they be done?" asked Hannah.

"They will be dry enough to fire in the kiln in a few days. Come, let us go over to the house. My wife will prepare the evening meal."

There were some large wooden doors that I hadn't noticed before because they were all the way open. Jairus pulled them closed and locked them. Then he turned and left the workshop from a smaller side door.

As Sarah, Noah, and Hannah followed him out, I looked more closely at the jugs that were drying. I reached out my finger and touched a jug carefully. It didn't feel like clay. It wasn't as soft as I expected. I touched it again, and then I pinched part of the handle between my fingers.

I'm not sure exactly what happened, but the handle came off and fell on the table.

I stepped away and looked to see if anyone had seen. No one was looking at me. Everyone had gone already, except Hannah, who had her back to me.

I followed her out and we went to Sarah's house.

Chapter Eight

One Broken Jug

We had dinner together and it was very good. I just couldn't enjoy it much because I was worried about the handle of the jug that I had broken.

"What's wrong, Caleb?" asked Hannah after dinner.

"Nothing," I said automatically. "Why?"

"You look worried, and you didn't eat very much."

"I'm fine," I said.

But later I kind of wished I had told Hannah the truth because I had a hard time falling asleep. We slept in a different little building than the one we had dinner in. Sarah said it was for guests. She slept with her parents in the room next to where we had eaten. We slept on mats on the floor, but that wasn't why I couldn't fall asleep. I kept thinking that I should have told Jairus what happened, but I was afraid he would be angry. I finally decided that I would tell him right away the next morning. Then I fell asleep.

But the next day, Jairus was already gone to work when we got up. After breakfast, we helped Sarah with some chores. We went with her to the market to get what her mother needed.

Sarah bought some fruit and vegetables. Then she went to a man selling barley. He had a scale there to weigh it, and he poured some on one side. The bowl went down and the empty one went up. Then he put one of his little metal weights on the other side. They almost balanced, but the barley side was a little higher, so the man poured more on the scale.

After Sarah paid and we were walking

away, Noah said, "I don't get what he did to make the two sides even."

So Sarah explained how the metal weights, like the ones I had seen when we first arrived, were used to balance a measure of barley that weighed the same amount as the weight.

"It is important that everyone has the same exact weights, so everyone gets the correct amount."

"Oh!" I said. "So that was why the man was doing an inspection yesterday."

"Yes. If a merchant used a weight that was less than it was supposed to be, he could cheat people by giving them less of the barley or whatever they were buying. So merchants can only use approved weights and scales."

As Sarah got the rest of the things she needed, Noah and I looked at cloth being sold. Soon Hannah came up to us, all excited.

"Guys, guess what I just heard?" she said.

At the same moment, Sarah also came over.

"I just heard that Jesus is heading toward Capernaum!" she said.

"Oh! So did I!" said Hannah.

"What?" I asked. "From where?"

"From Bethsaida," said Hannah.

"From Magdala," said Sarah at the same time.

The two girls looked at each other.

"Oh," said Sarah, looking disappointed. "They must just be rumors. I thought, because I heard it from the women talking by the well, that it might be true."

"I heard it from those people begging," said Hannah.

"They can't both be right," said Sarah.

"Let's go and see!" said Noah.

Even though I wanted so much to find Jesus, I suddenly thought that I didn't want to go yet, because I still had to tell Jairus about what I had done.

"I don't think we should just go running around after rumors," I said.

"Why not?" said Noah. "Let's just go to one of the towns and then the other."

"But they're in opposite directions," said Sarah. "That tells you that no one really knows. If it were two towns next to each other, it would be more likely to be true and not just a rumor."

Hannah agreed. Noah was disappointed, but I was glad.

"Okay, but we probably only have one more day here, right?" said Noah.

Hannah and I nodded. So far, on each of our adventures, we had always returned home on the "third day" as the people back then counted days, which was different from how we would count days. For example, on a Monday, *we* would say that Wednesday is two days away. But they would say that Wednesday is the third day from Monday.

After bringing Sarah's mom the things from the market, we went out to see Jairus digging some clay. It was along a stream that ran near the village and into the lake. Noah and I got to squish our hands and feet in the clay. It was neat to see how Jairus dug up slabs of it.

After lunch, we went with Sarah to her father's workshop. I was planning to tell him about the jug handle there, since it would be easier to be able to point to it and explain. But when we got there, there was another man with him. I was surprised to see that it was the merchant in colorful clothes I had watched the day before, when we first got to the market.

"Hello, my darling," said Jairus, giving Sarah a hug. "Hello, children. You may look around while I finish my business with Abner."

Jairus was showing Abner his finished jugs and bowls. Abner bought some of them and they wrapped them in material and put them in packs, like big backpacks.

I looked over to the place where the jugs were drying. I could see the jug that had only one handle, but from where I was standing, I couldn't see the handle that I had broken off.

"Did your father sell the little jars?" I asked Sarah. "I don't see them on the table there."

"No, those are for someone here in Capernaum," she answered. "He put them up on that shelf."

We looked where she was pointing and saw the five beautiful little jars on a shelf by themselves.

I watched and waited. I meant to tell Jairus about the jug handle as soon as Abner was gone. But Jairus walked out of the workshop with Abner and helped him load the packs on his donkey.

"Sarah, who is that man?" I asked. I had spotted the same old man with white curly hair again. He was standing near the kiln, watching Jairus and Abner. "I keep seeing him hanging around."

"That man?" said Sarah. "That is old Gilead. He comes here sometimes and Abba gives him alms. Abba says he is a blessing to us."

"Gives him what?" asked Noah.

"Alms," said Sarah. "You must know what alms are."

Noah looked at me and I looked at Hannah. Then we all looked at Sarah.

"Alms are when we give something to the poor, like money or food. It is a very good thing to do," explained Sarah.

"Oh, like a donation," said Noah.

"A what?" asked Sarah.

"Nothing, never mind," said Hannah. "Thank you for explaining. We do that too, of course."

"Sarah, my daughter," said Jairus as he came back in the shop, "run along with your friends. I must see to some business in the town."

Chapter Nine

Stolen Jars

It turned out that Abner was staying at Jairus's house, too. Sarah said she would sleep with us in the room where we ate dinner, and Abner would have the guest house.

At dinner that evening, I got a little bored listening to Jairus and Abner talk about trade routes and the costs of pottery.

I looked over at Sarah, who had helped her mother serve the dinner. I was thinking that maybe I should tell her about the jug I broke. She could go with me to tell her father. The only thing was, I didn't want her to know what

I had done because I didn't want her to think badly of me.

Suddenly Jairus stood up. I hadn't been paying attention to what they were saying.

"I must go to my workshop and get it right now," said Jairus. "You have never seen such detail on a simple bowl."

"No, my friend," said Abner. "You must certainly not go out now."

"Yes, I am going. I simply must show you this piece," said Jairus. "Please let me fill your glass. And have some more of these nuts. I will be back very soon."

Abner was smiling at Jairus, but as soon as he left, I noticed his face changed. He didn't look like he was happy about seeing this bowl or whatever it was. I was thinking that he probably wanted to go to bed like I did.

Jairus was not gone very long, but when he came back, he wasn't smiling either. He was holding one of the little jars he had shown us, and he was frowning. He stood in front of us, holding the jar.

"This is the only one left. The other four are missing," he said.

"Oh, Abba!" said Sarah. "Your special commission!"

"Someone has stolen them," said Jairus. "I looked all around to make sure they had not been knocked on the floor or moved somewhere else."

Abner came over and gently took the remaining jar from Jairus. He examined it closely.

"This is lovely work," he said. "Yes, it is a shame that the others are gone. Where did you keep them?"

"They were in my shop, as I said, on a little shelf behind my work area."

"Ah, I didn't notice them when I was there doing business with you. I'm surprised you didn't show them to me," said Abner.

"I didn't show them because they were not for sale," said Jairus.

"Yes, of course, you mentioned that they were made by special request. Well, they must have been stolen by someone who saw them and realized how valuable they are."

All through this conversation, I had been feeling more and more worried about the jug—

the one whose handle I broke. I still hadn't had a chance to tell Jairus what I had done and apologize. It seemed like this would be a really good time to do it.

I took a deep breath.

"Excuse me, sir?" I said.

Jairus looked at me.

"Yes?" he replied. "Did you see someone suspicious coming around my workshop?"

"I don't think so," I said. "I wanted to tell you about something else, though."

"Later, son," he said. "I need to get to the bottom of this."

"But, sir, I—I really should have said it before."

"Said what before?"

"Well, when you showed us around the day before yesterday, I really liked the shop and I wanted to feel the clay to find out what it felt like. So, I touched it."

"Caleb, that is fine. You did not touch my special little jars, did you?"

"No, sir. I touched one of the large jugs that was drying."

"That is fine, Caleb," he said. "Why are you telling me this?"

My throat felt so dry it was hard to talk. Jairus was looking at me funny. So was Abner. I didn't want to see what Sarah's face looked like.

"Well, when I touched it," I whispered, "the handle fell off. I'm sorry I broke it."

Chapter Ten

Wondering and Worrying

"Caleb, why didn't you say something?" said Hannah. "You should have told him right away."

"I know," I said. "I was afraid he would be angry."

"Caleb," said Jairus, frowning. "I am asking you: tell me the truth. Did you touch the little jars that I showed you?"

"No, sir!" I said. "Honestly, I didn't touch them. And I certainly didn't steal them. The last time I was in your workshop, they were there on the shelf."

I looked at his face and was afraid he didn't believe me. Just because I broke the jug, he was thinking that I had stolen from him!

"After what you have said, it is hard for me to believe that," said Jairus.

"I'm sorry about the broken jug," I said. "I don't have any money to pay for it, but I can do some chores for you."

"I am not concerned about the handle that fell off. You didn't break it. That can easily be reattached. And the fact that it fell off means I did not attach it well to begin with. So, if you had not knocked it off, it would have fallen off in the firing process."

Boy, was I glad to hear that!

"Caleb, someone who does something dishonest can very easily do other dishonest things. You did not tell me the truth right away about the handle. That was not honest."

My stomach felt funny when he said this. I knew that was true, but I also knew that I *was* being honest about the little jars. How could I get him to give me a second chance?

"Abba," said Sarah, "I am sure Caleb did

not steal from you. We have been together for the last two days and I know that he would not do that."

It made me feel good to hear Sarah say that, but it didn't seem like her father agreed.

"Hmph," said Jairus. "Right now I think we should just go to bed. In the morning we will look into this."

Jairus went off with Abner to show him his sleeping place, and Sarah got mats for us to sleep on.

"I can't believe you, Caleb," said Hannah, as we rolled out the mats. "Why in the world would you do that?"

"It was an accident, Hannah! I just wanted to touch it. I didn't think it would break. And when it did, I just panicked. I didn't want to get in trouble."

"Do not worry, Caleb," said Sarah. "It will be all right. I know that you are an honest boy."

"Thanks, Sarah," I said.

"I am wondering who it could have been, though. Who would steal from my father?"

"You know," I said. "There is something about Abner that makes me wonder."

"What do you mean?" asked Sarah.

"Well, I saw him at the market when we first arrived. And he did something that didn't seem right."

"What are you talking about, Caleb?" asked Hannah.

"Sarah, remember how you explained about the scales and weights needing to all be the same, so everything is fair? Well, right when we arrived, I saw a man inspecting Abner's weights and scales."

"There's nothing wrong with that," said Sarah. "They do it for everyone who sells at the market—local people and traveling merchants as well."

"Yes, but after that, a woman came to buy something, and Abner didn't use the weights the inspector had just checked."

"What?" said Sarah.

"I saw him. He took a weight from a little bag he had on his belt."

"That's right," said Hannah. "I remember you said something about it."

"Caleb, that means Abner is cheating," said Sarah. "There is no other reason to have two sets of weights. One of them must be lighter than the other. So, if the woman was paying for one measure of spices, she really received less than she paid for, because the weight would be lighter."

"Yes," said Hannah. "And as your father said, someone who does something dishonest can very easily do other dishonest things."

Jairus came back at that point and told us to turn out the lights and go to sleep. Actually, he didn't say "turn out the lights." He said "extinguish the lamp," but it means the same thing.

"Abba, first I must tell you something," said Sarah.

"What is it, my dear?"

"That man, Abner, is cheating in the marketplace. He has a double set of weights. I do not think he is an honest man."

"How do you know he has a double set of weights?"

"Caleb saw him," said Sarah.

"Ah. Caleb saw him. Thank you for letting me know, my darling. Now you must all go to bed."

We all lay down on sleeping mats with blankets over us. Jairus blew out the lamp and left.

"Thanks, Sarah," I said. "I don't think your father believed me, but thanks for sticking up for me."

"You are welcome," said Sarah. "I know none of you stole my father's little jars. I just hope he finds who did."

Chapter Eleven

Sounds in the Night

I don't know how long I had been asleep before I suddenly woke up. I lay still, trying to think of what had made me wake up. I listened but didn't hear anything. It was very quiet. Even where my family lives out in the country, it wasn't *this* quiet at night.

Just when I had started to fall asleep again, I heard something that made me fully awake. There was something or someone moving around in the courtyard.

My first thought was wolves, because on our first time-travel adventure, the wolves came out and surrounded us at night. But of course, that was outside the village of Bethlehem. I told myself that it couldn't be wolves in the court-yard in the middle of a town.

I listened for a while and heard more move-ments—like feet shuffling on the ground.

It was completely dark in the room. There were no streetlights outside to shine in the windows. Actually, there were no windows in the room we were in. I slowly crawled over to the door that led out to the courtyard. I didn't want to wake anyone up.

I stood up and carefully opened the door a tiny crack.

I couldn't see anything, but I heard more sounds that I couldn't identify. Then I heard something that sounded like a horse or a don-key blowing through its nose. Just when I was trying to remember if I had seen any animals in Jairus's yard before, there was another sound.

It was a man's voice. It was Abner.

"Come on, you stubborn animal!" he muttered.

Abner must be talking to his donkey. The

traveling merchants all use them. I remembered Levi telling us that on our last adventure. And of course Abner would have his donkey in the courtyard, since he was staying here.

But what would he be doing with it in the middle of the night?

I carefully opened the door wider. It made a small squeak. I stopped, and then pushed it a little more, so it was just wide enough for me to slip through.

Outside it was very dark, but not quite as dark as in the house. Looking up, I could see the outline of the house, but in the courtyard, everything was in shadow.

I stood still, listening, but didn't hear anything. Then there was the sound of the donkey breathing out of its nose again. I slowly stepped toward where the sound seemed to be coming from. As my eyes adjusted, I thought I could see the outline of the donkey.

Then, suddenly, I felt a hand grab my shoulder! I was too scared even to scream.

"Go back to bed, boy," Abner whispered in my ear. "You are not wanted here now."

He let go of my shoulder and moved away, toward his donkey. I was so terrified I couldn't move at first. Abner muttered something to his donkey and I heard the clipping sound of its hooves as it walked. I turned and ran back inside the house.

"Sarah! Wake up!" I whispered, reaching out to where I remembered her lying.

"Ah! What? What is it?"

"It's Abner. He's leaving. Right now. With his donkey!"

Sarah jumped up and ran into the other room.

"Abba! Imma!"

In a few seconds, everyone in the house was awake and out in the courtyard.

Well, it turned out all right because Jairus went running after Abner. I'm sure he realized that he was the thief, since he was taking off in the middle of the night. He didn't catch him, because Abner left his donkey and ran.

Jairus came back leading the donkey.

"Go to sleep, children. We will see tomorrow what tomorrow will bring."

The next morning, by the time we woke up, Jairus and Judith had already been up for a while. There was fresh bread with honey on it for breakfast. And Jairus had already unloaded the donkey and found the little jars, hidden deep in the bundles that were packed on the donkey's back.

He was very happy to have them, since he had promised to deliver them the next day.

As we ate breakfast, Jairus came over to me.

"Caleb, I want to thank you for your help in finding my jars. I am sorry that I suspected you."

"And I'm sorry that I touched your other jar without asking and broke it. And especially I'm sorry for not saying anything right away."

"Let us forgive each other, then," said Jairus. "My daughter Sarah will be very happy to know that we are at peace with each other."

"Okay!"

"You are welcome to stay however many days you like. I know that you are hoping that Jesus will come soon. I hope your prayers are answered."

"Thank you, sir," I said. "We're happy to stay with you and your wife and Sarah. Have you heard anything about Jesus coming?"

No sooner had I asked this, when someone came running to the door of the house and banged on it.

Jairus opened it.

"Jairus! He is here! Jesus is back!"

Sarah, Hannah, Noah, and I all jumped to our feet at the same time.

"Yay!" said Noah.

"Come on!" said Hannah.

"Wait!" cried Sarah.

"We have to hurry!" I said.

"But just let me tell you where—"

The three of us didn't pay attention to her. We knew that we didn't have much time. Today was the "third day."

We ran out the door and headed toward the house where Sarah had said Jesus stays every time he comes.

When we got there, I was surprised not to see anyone around.

"Don't you think there should be crowds of people?" I asked.

Hannah knocked on the door. No one answered and it was not locked, so she opened it a little.

"Hello?" said Hannah.

"Greetings and welcome," said a woman inside.

I looked around Hannah and saw two women preparing food.

"Oh," said Hannah. "Excuse us. We're looking for Jesus. We thought he would be here."

"Not yet," said the woman. "You will probably find him still on the way—either at the shore or in the marketplace. That is usually where all the sick line up and ask him to lay his hands on them."

"Come on, let's go! Quickly!" I said.

"Thank you," said Hannah. And we ran back out of the house.

We had only gone a few steps when the air seemed to become thick and we were moving in slow motion. And then, we were back. Back in our yard. Standing between the house and Dad's workshop.

Chapter Twelve

New Life

"Oh!" said Hannah.

"We were so close!" I said. "Just around the corner was the marketplace. Jesus was probably there healing people!"

"Why does this always happen?" asked Noah.

"I don't know," I said. "But we were *very* close. Maybe next time."

"What were we doing before we left, anyway?" asked Hannah.

"I don't remember," said Noah.

"You mean you can't remember what you were doing five minutes ago?" I said.

We all laughed, because it was days ago for us. But back here in our own time, only minutes had passed.

"Oh, I remember!" I said. "We were on our way to the workshop to see Dad's new puzzle."

That made us laugh more. It just seemed so funny that it was so hard to remember something that simple.

We went into the workshop and saw our dad sanding something on his bench.

"Hi, Dad!" said Noah. "It's so good to see you!" He ran over and hugged him.

"Well, hi, Noah. It's good to see you, too. I haven't seen you since, what, lunchtime?"

"Yeah, but it's always nice to see you, Dad. I like coming to your workshop and trying out the toys you make."

"I'm glad to hear it, Noah. What do you think of this?"

He held up something that looked like a little treasure chest, except it had pieces that slid into place like a 3-D puzzle.

"Cool!" I said.

Noah and I were still trying to put the pieces back together, when Dad's cell phone beeped. He looked at the text message, which was almost always from Mom.

"Caleb, run over to the house. Your mom says your friend Kevin is on the phone for you."

"Aw, Dad, I don't want to talk to Kevin. He ruined our project again."

Dad just gave me a look, so I left and went over to the house. As I walked, I thought about telling my mom that I wouldn't talk to him because I was too mad. But then I remembered how it felt when someone wouldn't listen to me, even though I was telling the truth. I thought that maybe I should give Kevin a chance to explain.

"Oh, Caleb," my mom said as I came in the kitchen door. "The phone's for you. It's Kevin."

I picked up the phone.

"Hi, Kevin," I said.

"Caleb! I'm sorry about the rocket. I really didn't mean to let it get wrecked. My baby sister got it and pulled off the fins and smashed it a little. I'm working on fixing it."

My little brother Noah was older than Kevin's baby sister, but I remembered times when he was littler and he would grab things and destroy them before anyone could stop him.

"That's all right, Kevin. I mean, I was mad when I heard about it, but I understand about little sisters."

"Oh, thanks, Caleb. You know, if you come over and help me, I think we could get it fixed before the deadline on Tuesday."

"I'll ask my mom if I can come over. Just a second." I covered the phone with my hand. "Mom, can you take me over to Kevin's house sometime so we can fix the rocket?"

She ended up driving me over on Saturday, and we worked on the rocket and made it even better than before.

The next day was Sunday, so we went to Mass. Kevin's family was already there. I smiled at him as we walked down the aisle and sat in another pew.

Mass began like usual, but right at the beginning, I heard something I had never noticed before. It was during the part when we think about our sins and tell God we are sorry. Father Joe said, "Lord Jesus, you raise us to new life." We all responded, "Lord, have mercy." But I was surprised by that "raised to new life" part. It made me think of Sarah. Jesus *had* raised her, but when did he raise me to new life?

Then, during the homily, Father Joe talked about what people said in the Gospel story. I didn't get the whole thing, but Jesus was teaching in Nazareth, where he was from. The people said, "Isn't this the carpenter, the son of Mary?"

"The people of the town had watched Jesus grow up," said Father Joe. "He seemed like a regular boy to them. And he had become the village carpenter after Joseph, his foster father, had died. So they expected him to act like a carpenter, not a teacher or prophet. They were not happy with him, and they didn't believe he could do any miracles and mighty deeds for them. Imagine what life could have been like for them if they had given him the chance."

That made me think of how I got mad at Kevin, and then how I gave him a chance to explain. And I was so glad that I did, because Kevin and I were even better friends now.

Then I realized that this is probably what being "raised to new life" means. It's not like we are actually dead. But new life means being forgiven or having another chance. And God does that for us at Mass, when we go to confession, and just every day!

"Thank you, Jesus!" I prayed. "Thank you for new life. Thank you for my friend Kevin. Thank you!"

Where Is It in the Bible?

The story of Jesus raising the daughter of Jairus from the dead is told in both the Gospel according to Mark and the Gospel according to Luke. (There is a short version in the Gospel according to Matthew.) They mention only the father's name, Jairus. The Bible doesn't tell us the name of the girl or her mother, or what Jairus did for a living. This story is interesting because it is a story within a story. Notice how the story of this miracle is interrupted to tell the story of another miracle. Here is the version in the Gospel according to Mark:

When Jesus had crossed again in the boat to the other side, a great crowd gathered around him; and he was by the sea. Then one of the leaders of the synagogue named Jairus came and, when he saw him, fell at his feet and begged him repeatedly, "My little daughter is at the point of death. Come and lay your hands on her, so that she may be made well, and live."

So he went with him. And a large crowd followed him and pressed in on him. Now there was a woman who had been suffering from hemorrhages for twelve years. She had endured much under many physicians, and had spent all that she had; and she was no better, but rather grew worse. She had heard about Jesus, and came up behind him in the crowd and touched his cloak, for she said, "If I but touch his clothes, I will be made well." Immediately her hemorrhage stopped; and she felt in her body that she was healed of her disease. Immediately aware that power had gone forth from him, Jesus turned about in the crowd and said, "Who touched my clothes?" And his disciples said to him, "You see the crowd pressing in on you; how can you say, 'Who touched me?'" He looked all round to see who had done it. But the woman, knowing what had happened to her, came in fear and trembling, fell down before him, and told him the whole truth. He said to her, "Daughter, your faith has made you well; go in peace, and be healed of your disease."

While he was still speaking, some people came from the leader's house to say, "Your daughter is dead. Why trouble the teacher any further?" But overhearing what they said, Jesus said to the leader of the synagogue, "Do not fear, only believe." He allowed no one to follow him except Peter, James, and John, the brother of James. When they came to the house of the leader of the synagogue, he saw a commotion, people weeping and wailing loudly. When he had entered, he said to them, "Why do you make a commotion and weep? The child is not dead but sleeping." And they laughed at him. Then he put them all out-side, and took the child's father and moth-er and those who were with him, and went in where the child was. He took her by the hand and said to her, "Talitha cum," which means, "Little girl, get up!" And immediate-ly the girl got up and began to walk about (she was twelve years of age). At this they were overcome with amazement. He strict-ly ordered them that no one should know this, and told them to give her something to eat (Mark 5:21–43).

Gospel TimeTrekkers

Written by Maria Grace Dateno, FSP
Illustrated by Paul Cunningham

Three
ordinary kids,
six extraordinary
adventures,
one incredible quest!

Join Caleb, Hannah, and Noah as they're whisked away to the time of Jesus and find themselves immersed in some of the most amazing Bible stories of all!

Who are the Daughters of St. Paul?

We are Catholic sisters. Our mission is to be like Saint Paul and tell everyone about Jesus! There are so many ways for people to communicate with each other. We want to use all of them so everyone will know how much God loves us. We do this by printing books (you're holding one!), making radio shows, singing, helping people at our bookstores, using the Internet, and in many other ways.

Visit our Web site at www.pauline.org

BOOKS & MEDIA

The Daughters of St. Paul operate book and media centers at the following addresses. Visit, call, or write the one nearest you today, or find us at www.paulinestore.org.

CALIFORNIA
3908 Sepulveda Blvd, Culver City, CA 90230 — 310-397-8676
3250 Middlefield Road, Menlo Park, CA 94025 — 650-369-4230

FLORIDA
145 S.W. 107th Avenue, Miami, FL 33174 — 305-559-6715

HAWAII
1143 Bishop Street, Honolulu, HI 96813 — 808-521-2731

ILLINOIS
172 North Michigan Avenue, Chicago, IL 60601 — 312-346-4228

LOUISIANA
4403 Veterans Memorial Blvd, Metairie, LA 70006 — 504-887-7631

MASSACHUSETTS
885 Providence Hwy, Dedham, MA 02026 — 781-326-5385

MISSOURI
9804 Watson Road, St. Louis, MO 63126 — 314-965-3512

NEW YORK
64 W. 38th Street, New York, NY 10018 — 212-754-1110

SOUTH CAROLINA
243 King Street, Charleston, SC 29401 — 843-577-0175

TEXAS
Currently no book center; for parish exhibits or outreach evangelization, contact: 210-569-0500, or SanAntonio@paulinemedia.com, or P.O. Box 761416, San Antonio, TX 78245

VIRGINIA
1025 King Street, Alexandria, VA 22314 — 703-549-3806

CANADA
3022 Dufferin Street, Toronto, ON M6B 3T5 — 416-781-9131

¡También somos su fuente para libros,
videos y música en español!